MAJOR LEAGUE SPORTS

MAJOR LEAGUE BASEBALL

By Kevin Frederickson

Kaleidoscope
Minneapolis, MN

Your Front Row Seat to the Games

This edition first published in 2020 by Kaleidoscope Publishing, Inc.

For information regarding permission, write to
Kaleidoscope Publishing, Inc.
6012 Blue Circle Drive
Minnetonka, MN 55343

Library of Congress Control Number
2019939022

ISBN
978-1-64519-069-1 (library bound)
978-1-64494-158-4 (paperback)
978-1-64519-170-4 (ebook)

Printed in the United States of America.

TABLE OF CONTENTS

CHAPTER 1

A Great Day for a Ballgame

The green grass is freshly cut. The brown dirt is smooth. The sun shines bright. It's a beautiful summer day for baseball.

Rick Porcello pitches for the Boston Red Sox against the Houston Astros.

Thousands of fans arrive at Minute Maid Park. Many wear baseball caps. Some wear jerseys. One fan sips a soda. Another is eating a hot dog. They are ready to cheer on the home team, the Houston Astros.

The Major League Baseball (MLB) season lasts 162 games. That means each team hosts half that many, or 81. The season starts in spring. It ends in the fall. Early and late games are sometimes played in cold weather. But most baseball games are in the summer. For many fans, baseball is a summer **tradition**.

Houston Astros batter Jose Altuve awaits a pitch against the Boston Red Sox.

The Astros are hosting the Boston Red Sox. Rick Porcello is on the mound for Boston. He leans over. The catcher points down with one finger. That tells Porcello what pitch to throw. He begins his windup. Astros hitter Jose Altuve bends his knees. He adjusts his weight. Then he swings.

Crack!

The ball smacks off the wooden bat. Altuve watches it soar high. The Boston outfielders run after it. Finally, they stop. They know they can't catch it. The ball lands over the fence. Home run!

The fans stand up to cheer. Altuve takes his time running around the bases. He reaches third base. A coach gives him a high-five. Then, Altuve steps on home plate. He has just completed one of the most exciting plays in baseball.

FUN FACT

Until interleague play began in 1997, teams from the American League and National League could only meet in the World Series.

Major League Baseball Map

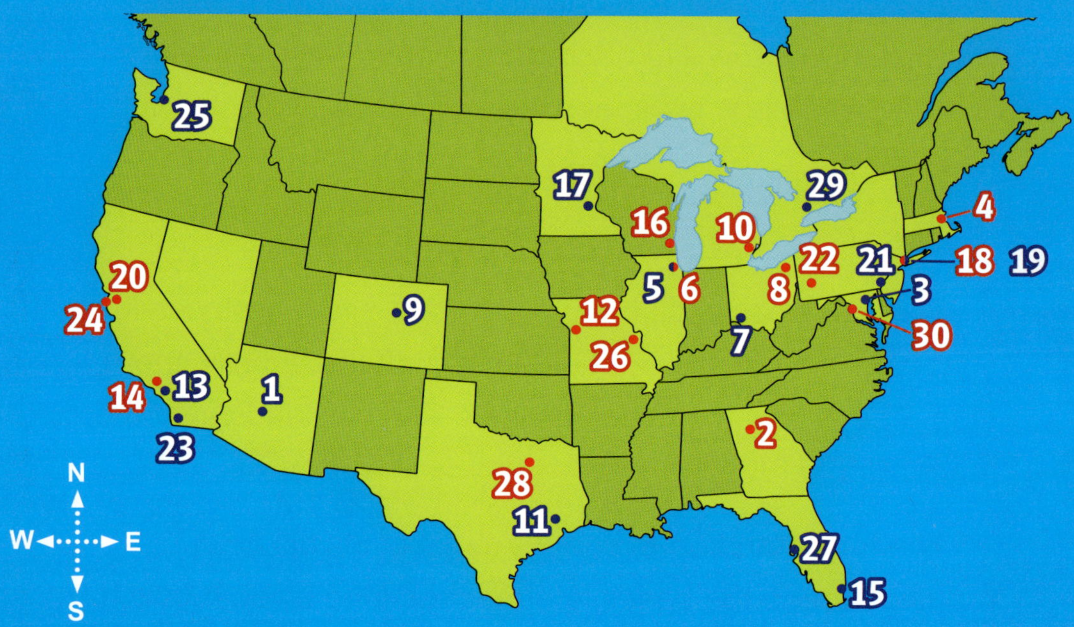

1. Arizona Diamondbacks
2. Atlanta Braves
3. Baltimore Orioles
4. Boston Red Sox
5. Chicago Cubs
6. Chicago White Sox
7. Cincinnati Reds
8. Cleveland Indians
9. Colorado Rockies
10. Detroit Tigers
11. Houston Astros
12. Kansas City Royals
13. Los Angeles Angels
14. Los Angeles Dodgers
15. Miami Marlins
16. Milwaukee Brewers
17. Minnesota Twins
18. New York Mets
19. New York Yankees
20. Oakland Athletics
21. Philadelphia Phillies
22. Pittsburgh Pirates
23. San Diego Padres
24. San Francisco Giants
25. Seattle Mariners
26. St. Louis Cardinals
27. Tampa Bay Rays
28. Texas Rangers
29. Toronto Blue Jays
30. Washington Nationals

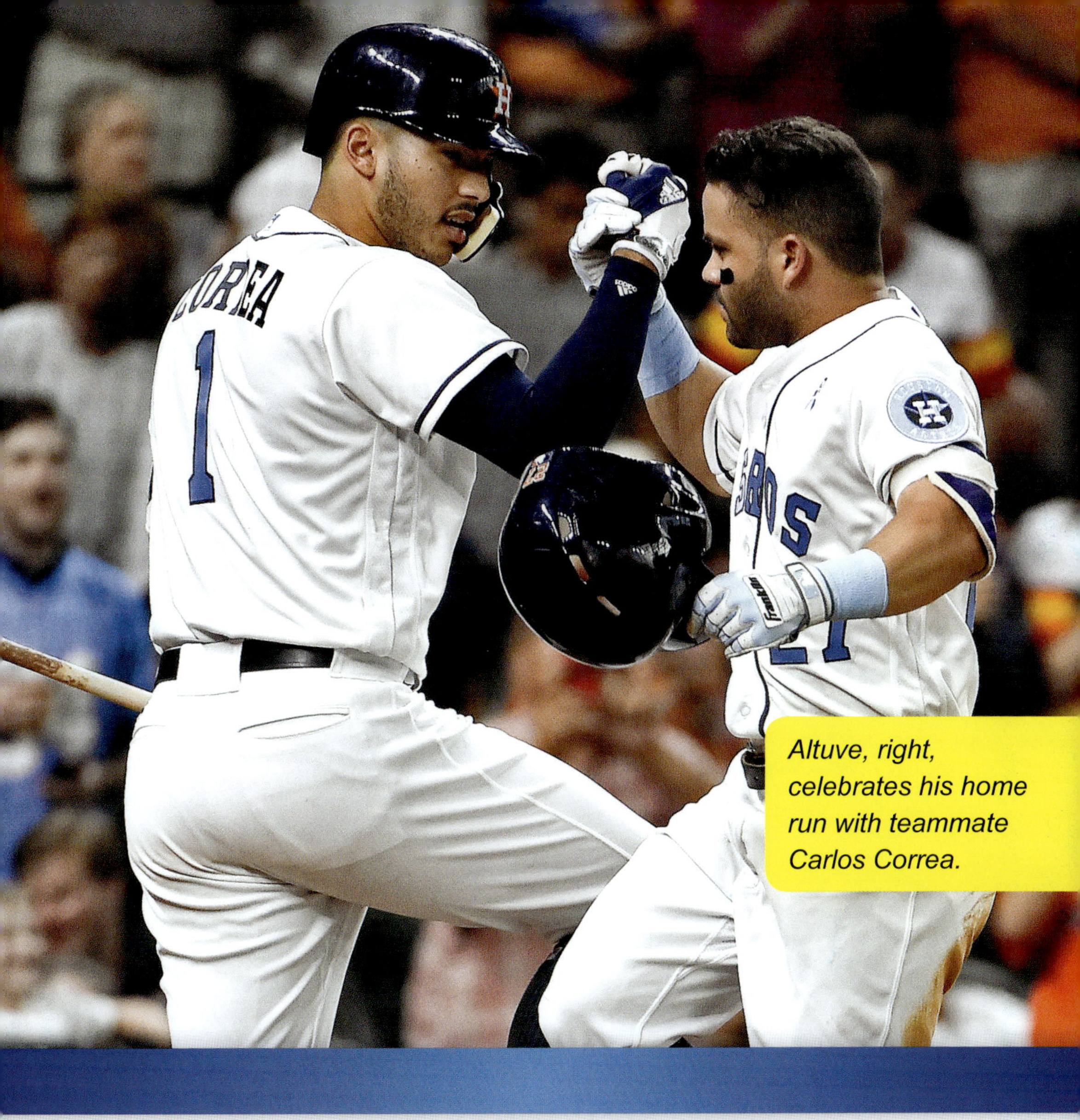

Altuve, right, celebrates his home run with teammate Carlos Correa.

Baseball has been around since the mid-1800s. The sport is still popular today. Teams now play in fancy ballparks. Players earn millions of dollars each year. And thousands of fans attend each game. But fans have been cheering for plays just like Altuve's for more than a century. That's just one part of what makes baseball so special.

CHAPTER 2

America's Pastime

Fans arrive at the ballpark. The men wear suits. Women are in dresses. No one has a ball cap on. Instead, the men wear fancy hats. After all, this is a special **occasion**.

Fans fill in Huntington Avenue Baseball Grounds for Game 1 of the 1903 World Series.

It's October 1903. The fans are at Boston's Huntington Avenue Baseball Grounds. And the Boston Americans are hosting the Pittsburgh Pirates. This is the first World Series.

BASEBALL FIELD

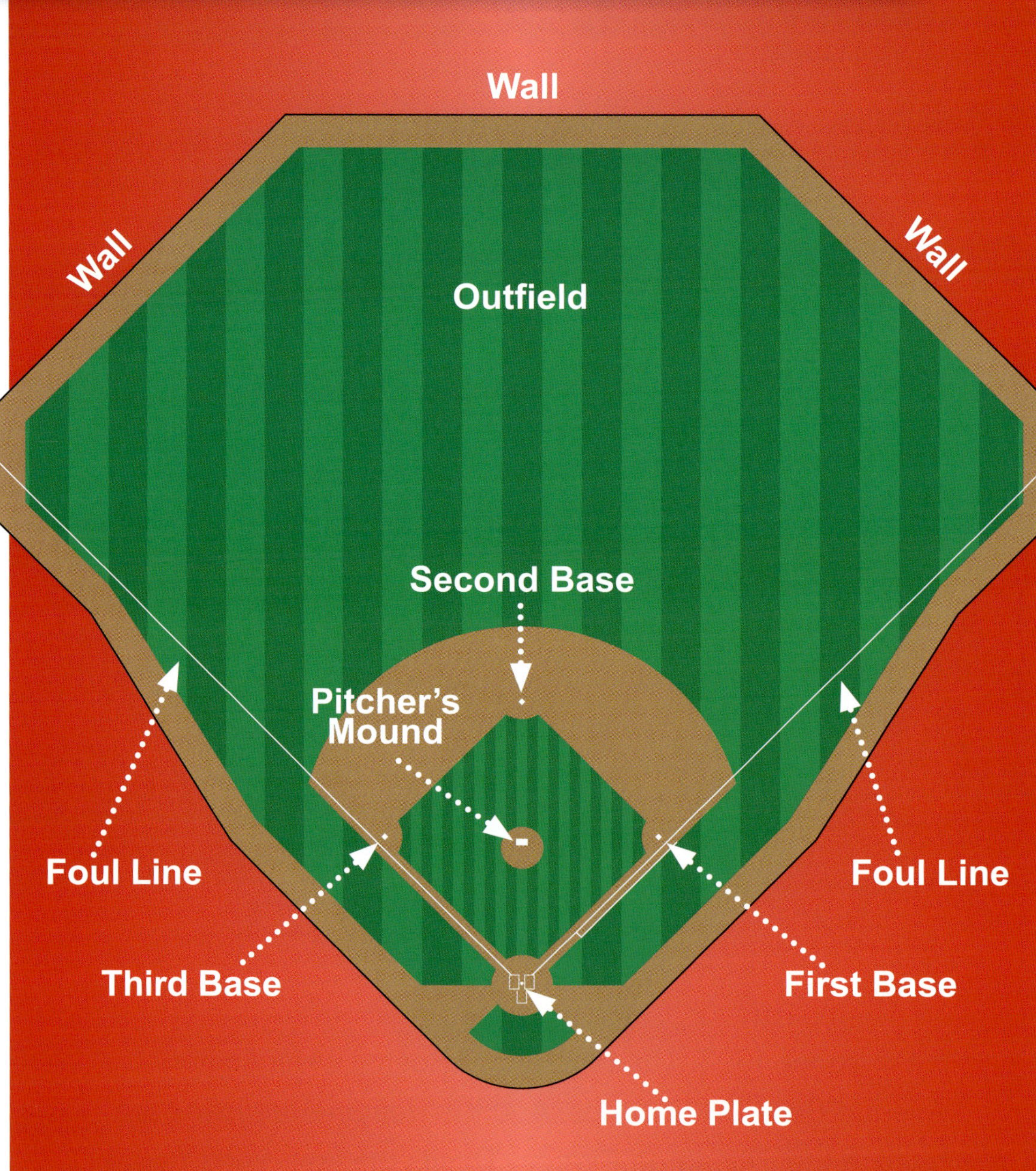

The clothes weren't the only thing different in 1903. Crowds were smaller. Most games had only 16,000 fans or so. Fans usually paid less than one dollar for a ticket. And following from home was much harder. There was no TV. There was no radio, either. But print reporters covered the game. Fans could read more about it in the newspaper.

The Americans won that first World Series. Today they are the Red Sox. Much more has changed since 1903. Back then, MLB had sixteen teams. None were west of St. Louis. Today there are thirty teams. They play in cities across the country. One even plays in Canada.

BEFORE THE WORLD SERIES

Harry Wright crosses the plate. His cap is red. He's wearing a white jersey. A big red C is over his chest. Wright plays for the Cincinnati Red Stockings. They won their first game 45–9 in 1869. The Red Stockings were the first professional baseball team. They eventually became today's Cincinnati Reds.

In 1903, fans waited a long time for runs to score. Pitchers dominated the game. That period is now called the Deadball **Era**. In other eras, hitters had their way. Fans wanted to watch them hit home runs.

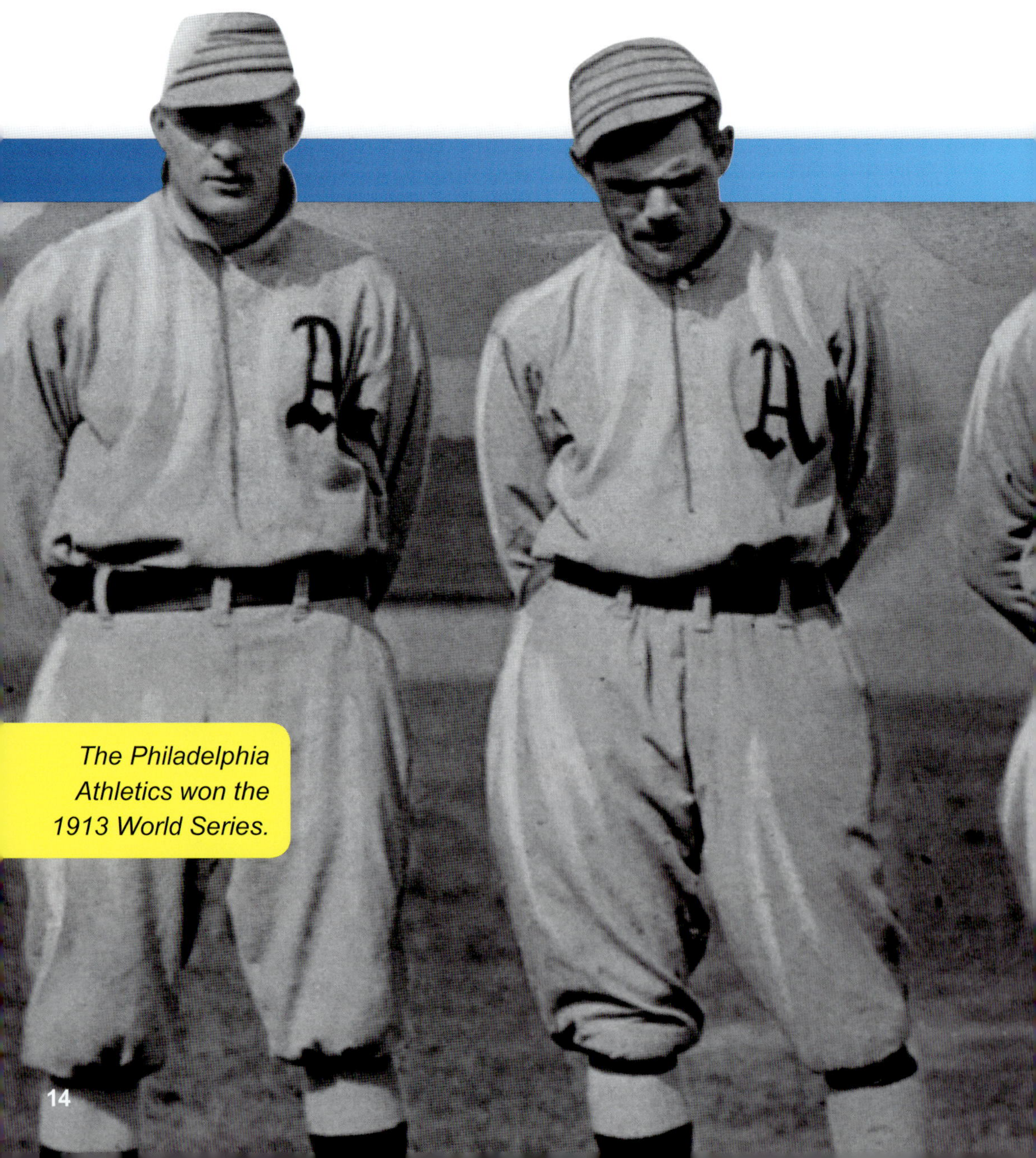

The Philadelphia Athletics won the 1913 World Series.

Much in baseball has changed over the years. But much has also stayed the same. The rules are mostly unchanged. Records last for years. Fans love spending summer days at ballparks. And just like in 1903, the World Series is still a special occasion.

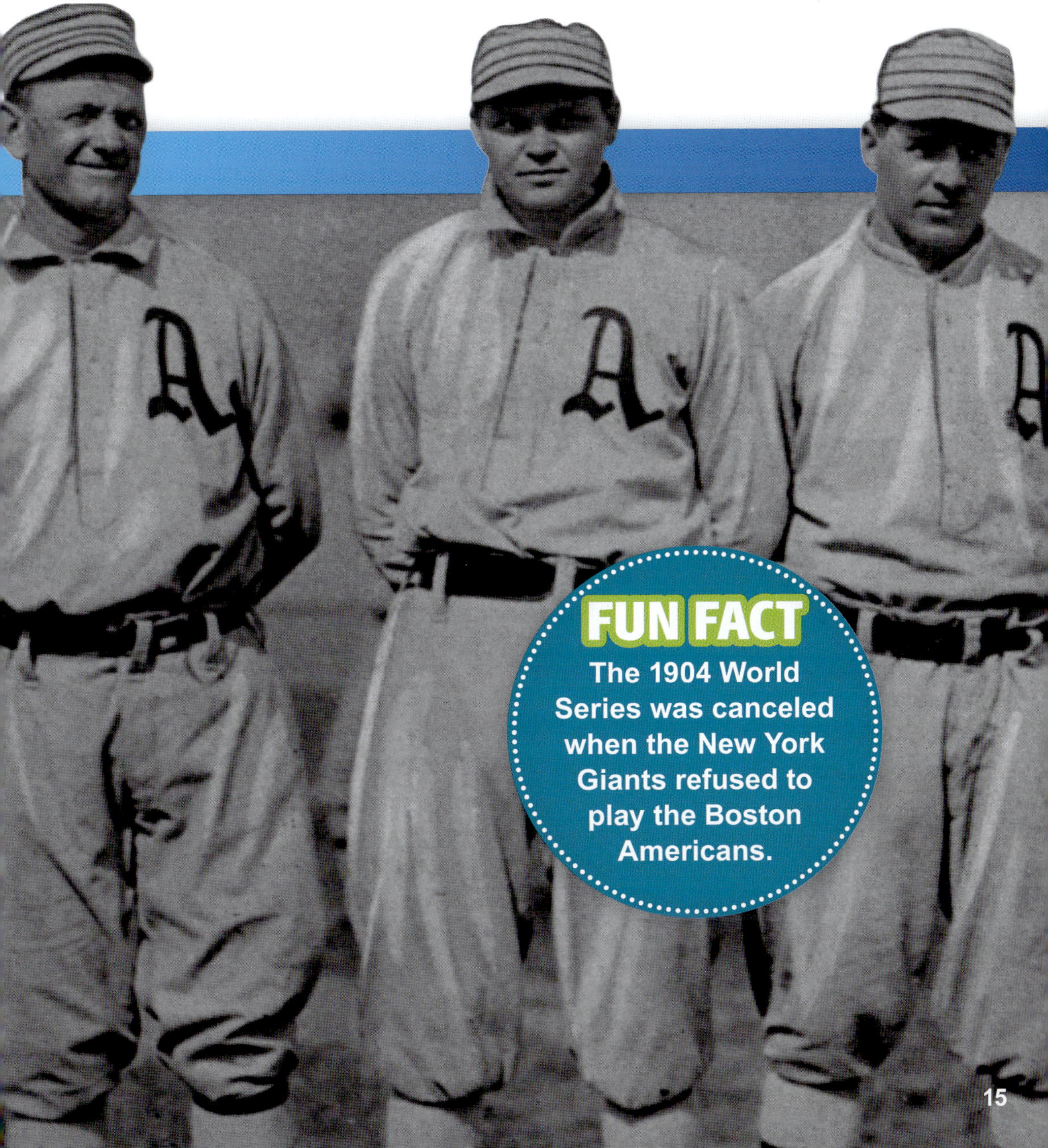

FUN FACT
The 1904 World Series was canceled when the New York Giants refused to play the Boston Americans.

CHAPTER 3

Shining Stars

Mariano Rivera stands on the dirt mound. He takes a deep breath. Rivera is a **closer**. The New York Yankees call on him to finish games. Now Rivera needs to get just one more out. If he can, the Yankees win the 2009 World Series.

Rivera fires off a pitch. The Philadelphia Phillies hitter makes contact. Barely. The ball rolls to the Yankees' second baseman. He fires it to first. It's an easy out. New York has won its twenty-seventh World Series. No team has won close to as many. The St. Louis Cardinals rank second. They won their eleventh title in 2011.

FUN FACT

Yankees catcher Yogi Berra won a record 10 World Series from 1947 to 1962.

Mariano Rivera pitches with the championship on the line in the 2009 World Series.

The Yankees' first championship came in 1923. It signaled the beginning of a new era. Pitchers had ruled in the early 1900s. Walter Johnson became famous for getting strikeout after strikeout. Babe Ruth changed everything. The Yankees' slugger hit many home runs. Fans couldn't get enough of Ruth. He became the game's home run king. Soon, power hitters ruled the game.

Willie Mays was baseball's do-it-all star for the Giants from 1951 to 1972.

Ruth's skills also impacted the Yankees. He led them to three more World Series wins through 1932. Many say the 1927 Yankees were the best team ever.

More superstars followed Ruth. Jackie Robinson starred for the Brooklyn Dodgers. Robinson **debuted** in 1947. MLB had previously refused black players. Robinson opened the door for more black stars. Willie Mays was one of them. He roamed center field for the New York Giants. Then the team moved to San Francisco. That's where Mays became one of the sport's all-around best players.

Jackie Robinson

FENWAY PARK

HOME OF THE BOSTON RED SOX

Built: 1912

Fenway Park hosted its first game on April 20, 1912. This makes it the oldest stadium in baseball.

Cost: $650,000

The ballpark was rebuilt in 1934. In the early 2000s, it underwent a $285 million renovation.

Capacity: 37,755

Only three MLB stadiums seat fewer people. Dodger Stadium in Los Angeles is the biggest, seating 56,000 fans.

Feature: The Green Monster

The left-field wall at Fenway is 37 feet (11 m) tall. Built in 1934, this wall is nicknamed "The Green Monster."

Great hitters get a lot of attention. Players like Ruth, Hank Aaron, and Alex Rodriguez hit lots of home runs. Ichiro Suzuki had a different style. He hit to the gaps. Then he raced quickly around the bases.

Pitchers have unique styles, too. Johnson and Cy Young threw the ball hard in baseball's early years. Sandy Koufax ruled the 1960s. He had a blazing fastball. Koufax threw a tricky curveball, too. Today Max Scherzer is a star. He mixes up five strong pitches.

Max Scherzer combines power and precision when pitching for the Washington Nationals.

CHAPTER 4

A Global Game

Brown dirt fills the diamond. But it is uneven. Pebbles are scattered throughout the infield. The grass in the outfield is long. Weeds are creeping up. But the players do not care. They run to their positions. Baseball is a way of life in the Dominican Republic. Kids love to play. And some of them become really good. Sluggers such as David Ortiz and Albert Pujols are among the stars who grew up there.

Baseball is called America's pastime. Today the sport is growing all over the world.

Kids in the Dominican Republic take part in a baseball camp.

Many people in Latin America love baseball. The Dominican Republic has lots of baseball. The sport is big in Cuba, Puerto Rico, and Venezuela, too. MLB is the world's most popular baseball league. The next biggest league is in Japan. South Korea has a growing league as well.

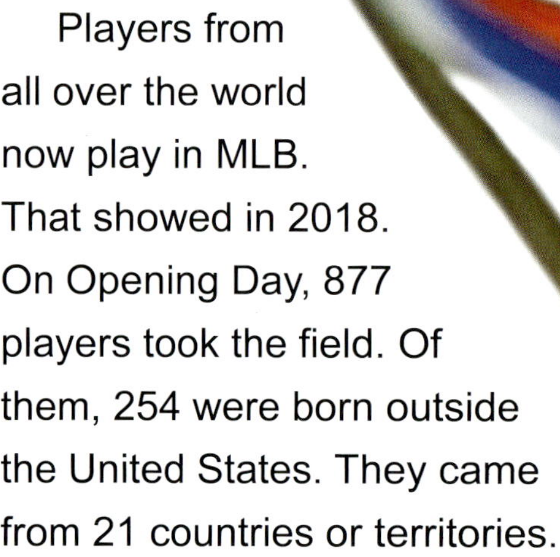

Players from all over the world now play in MLB. That showed in 2018. On Opening Day, 877 players took the field. Of them, 254 were born outside the United States. They came from 21 countries or territories.

Sometimes players represent their countries. Francisco Lindor and Carlos Correa enter Dodger Stadium. They are MLB stars. In this game, they are playing for Team Puerto Rico. It's the 2017 World Baseball Classic final. This event features national teams.

FUN FACT

Japan won the first two World Baseball Classics, in 2006 and 2009.

Fans of Puerto Rico's team cheer on the squad at the World Baseball Classic.

Technology is helping baseball move into the future.

Technology has helped the game grow. One fan listens to the Dodgers on the radio. He lives near Dodger Stadium in Los Angeles. A fan in New York watches on TV. Another fan in South Korea streams the game online. Fans in Japan and Puerto Rico discuss the game on social media.

Fans have more information than ever. The strike zone can be shown on a TV screen. Stats are beamed around the world instantly. Now some calls can even be reviewed. **Umpires** use instant replay.

Not all fans agree with these changes. They would like baseball to stay the same. But others are excited to see the sport changing with the times. Either way, baseball is an old-fashioned game with a bright future.

FUN FACT

Until 1955, no MLB team existed west of St. Louis.

BEYOND THE BOOK

After reading the book, it's time to think about what you learned. Try the following exercises to jumpstart your ideas.

THINK

DIFFERENT SOURCES. What kind of sources could you use to find out more information on MLB? How could each source be useful?

CREATE

SHARPEN YOUR RESEARCH SKILLS. Where could you go to find out more information about the Cincinnati Red Stockings? Find out more about this team, create a research plan, and write a paragraph about what your next steps would be.

SHARE

SUM IT UP. Write a paragraph about the most important topics in this book. Use your own words. Do not copy from the book. Then, share the paragraph with a classmate. What does your classmate think of your paragraph? Does he or she have any questions for you about MLB?

GROW

DRAWING CONNECTIONS. Create a diagram that shows how MLB connects with math. How do you think math can help players and coaches win games? How does learning about math help you better understand MLB?

Visit www.ninjaresearcher.com/0691 to learn how to take your research skills and book report writing to the next level!

RESEARCH

SEARCH LIKE A PRO

Learn about how to use search engines to find useful websites.

FACT OR FAKE?

Discover how you can tell a trusted website from an untrustworthy resource.

TEXT DETECTIVE

Explore how to zero in on the information you need most.

SHOW YOUR WORK

Research responsibly—learn how to cite sources.

WRITE

GET TO THE POINT

Learn how to express your main ideas.

PLAN OF ATTACK

Learn prewriting exercises and create an outline.

DOWNLOADABLE REPORT FORMS

Further Resources

BOOKS

Bechtel, Mark. *Sports Illustrated Kids Big Book of Who: Baseball.* Liberty Street, 2017.

Lyon, Drew. *Superfan's Guide to Pro Baseball Teams.* Capstone Press, 2018.

Mason, Tyler. *12 Reasons to Love Baseball.* 12-Story Library, 2018.

WEBSITES

Factsurfer.com gives you a safe, fun way to find more information.

1. Go to www.factsurfer.com.
2. Enter "Major League Baseball" into the search box and click 🔍.
3. Select your book cover to see a list of related websites.

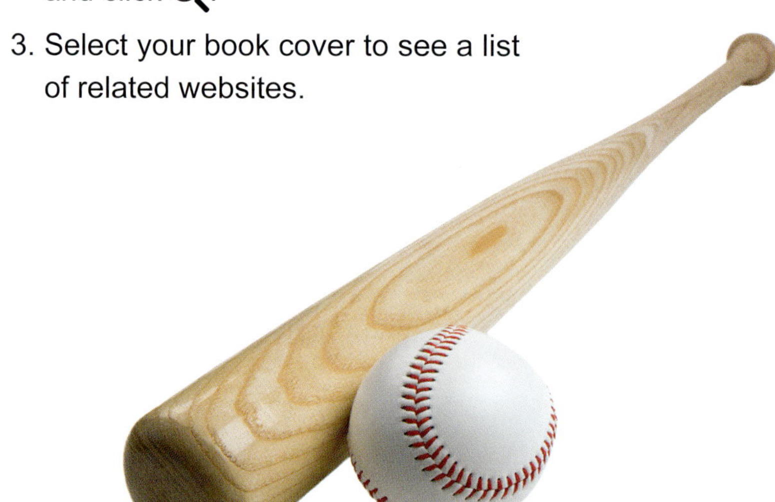

Glossary

closer: A closer is a pitcher who comes in at the end of games. Mariano Rivera was the Yankees' star closer.

debut: A debut is when somebody does something for the first time. Jackie Robinson debuted for the Dodgers in 1947.

era: An era is a period of time. The Deadball Era in baseball happened in the early 1900s.

occasion: An occasion is a special event. The World Series is a special occasion each year for baseball fans.

professional: Professional means to be paid for doing something. All MLB players are professionals.

technology: Technology is something created using science. Technology is changing the ways baseball is played and watched.

tradition: A tradition is something people do over and over. For many people baseball is a summer tradition.

umpire: An umpire upholds the rules during a baseball game. The umpire said the player was out after being tagged.

Index

PHOTO CREDITS

The images in this book are reproduced through the courtesy of: Louis Lopez/Cal Sport Media/AP Images, front cover (center); Eugene Onischenko/Shutterstock Images, front cover (background); Keeton Gale/Shutterstock Images, p. 3; Juan DeLeon/Icon Sportswire/AP Images, p. 4; Felix Mizioznikov/Shutterstock Images, p. 5; Chris Brown/Cal Sport Media/AP Images, p. 6; Ruksutakarn studio/Shutterstock Images, p. 7; Red Line Editorial, p. 8; Eric Christian Smith/ AP Images, p. 9; AP Images, pp. 10–11, 14–15, 16; Dejan Popovic/Shutterstock Images, p. 12; Elise Amendola/AP Images, pp. 16–17; Robert H. Houston/AP Images, pp. 18–19; catwalker/ Shutterstock Images, p. 19; Jason Tench/Shutterstock Images, p. 20 (field); Alex Brandon/AP Images, p. 21; Ramon Espinosa/AP Images, pp. 22–23; Alan C. Heison/Shutterstock Images, p. 24; Ricardo Arduengo/AP Images, pp. 24–25; Gene J. Puskar/AP Images, p. 26; Frank Romeo/Shutterstock Images, p. 27; photastic/Shutterstock Images, p. 30.

ABOUT THE AUTHOR

Kevin Frederickson is a freelance writer and editor from Ohio. He lives near Cincinnati with his golden doodle, Max.